The Sparkle Tree

Dr. Stefenie R. Lott

DEDICATION

Because of his everlasting love, protection and provision, I dedicate this book to God. You have sparked creativity in me and given me the ability to get wealth. To you, my heavenly Father and to you only do I dedicate the mind and strength to write this book.

TABLE OF CONTENTS

ACKNOWLEDGMENTS

I thank my God for his guidance and patience with me in doing what he has commanded me to do. I give honor to my husband who is also my pastor. He constantly tells me that I can do whatever I put my mind to. The time that he allows me to express my creativity is awesome. My children, biological or otherwise, siblings and church family, you rock! Thanks for your support in whatever avenue I decide to travel. You are always here for me. Thanks for helping me stay focused on the Vision. Truly not least, my Facebook family, thanks for your support. Thanks for the likes and comments through the years.

The Sparkle Tree

Chapter 1

Visiting Grandma

I remember, like it was yesterday, visiting my grandma. My sister and I were always looking forward to any breaks from school, but especially summer break. Summer break was the longest, which made it the best. The things that we could do at grandma's house were so much better than what we could ever think of doing at home. At home we could play in the front or back yard or even down the street, but at our grandma's house, play turned into adventure. Make believe was awesome!

Our grandma lived in sort of a rural area. There was a lot of open space, with few cars passing through and plenty of grass and dirt, of course. Space to run and jump and flip and spin! We loved every minute of it. There weren't many neighbors who lived close to my grandma. There were neighbors, but a long way down the road. Yes, road, not the street. It was a rock road, as we called it, but rather gravel road. So, there were no other children in the close vicinity of where my grandma lived. When we returned home, we would sit with friends and tell them all about our visit each time we went to visit grandma, especially Zion Michelle and Mary Micah, we all were best of friends. It appears they could feel the enthusiasm that was exuding from us as we told of the events that transpired in each of our visits.

Of all the events that we encountered during our many visits, there was one that we never shared. I don't know if we didn't believe it or understand what we saw or if our eyes were playing a trick on us. I know, both of us shouldn't have our eyes playing tricks on us at the same time for the same thing. But what we saw was so amazingly beautiful. So, calming. Yet, we never went to see where it was coming from. At night we would just look out of the window or stand on the porch, hoping that it would appear. Just like clockwork, it was always there. The light came from the woods. I don't know how close or far away it was, I only know that it was. It was always a pleasing sight to watch.

For as long as we visited our grandma, the light was there. I never remember the woods being dark, without the light. From my youth, there was always a light in the woods. It wasn't always bright light, but it was a light and at times it did sort of glimmer. There was a time that I thought it was a fire, but there was no smoke and it never got any larger nor was there the smell of anything burning. For a long time, I wondered why the light was there. One day I finally asked my grandma what was this light in the woods? My grandma told us a story about a tree that would sparkle in the deep woods. I asked her why a tree would sparkle, and she said that trees were alive and have feelings and could also feel how people feel. I didn't understand how a tree could feel. But I accepted what my grandma said. I told her that we, my sister and I, would just sit and watch the woods for hours looking at the lights, just wondering about the lights in the woods. Many days we would walk to the edge of the woods, just far enough so that our grandma could still see us. But I had never been that deep into the woods to see the tree that sparkled, but I could see the light from my window or the front porch. We would watch that light so long, that grandma would have to make us go to bed. It was such a soothing sight. It was almost like listening to a lullaby as you're being rocked to sleep.

My grandma said that when she was a little girl, the light would change color. At that time, she lived many miles from the woods. She said that sometimes the colors would be green, or blue, red, pink, bright orange. I asked her, why did the tree change color? She said that she was told that many people would bring their problems to the tree and the tree would make them feel better by changing colors as the people sat and gave deep thought to the troubles they were experiencing. She said that the people would talk to the tree and laugh as they shared their circumstances with the tree. It was like they were old friends. People spent a lot of time pouring their problems out on the tree. After they poured out, it was as if they would receive comfort from the tree. They would enjoy the beautiful flowers surrounding the tree, then all would seem well. Then at night they would watch the colors from almost anywhere. My grandma said the tree was like therapy. It seemed to make the world better for some people.

Grandma said that at one time the light was extremely bright. She said that you could see the light radiate and dance far above the other trees in the woods. It was almost like a rainbow over the woods, sparkling, a ribbon of color dancing in the air. She couldn't remember, at that time, when the tree did not sparkle. She could only remember the intensity of the light and how the light danced in the darkness. She said that it would bring joy to her heart.

.

Chapter 2

Grandma's Discovery

She remembers the time when her husband died, my grandpa, I was only a baby. She said that she was depressed, didn't know what she would do or where she would go. He bought this house for them. They were to spend the rest of their lives here together. She told me that she would sit for hours just watching the woods at night. Watching the lights as they flickered and changed to an assortment of colors. She said oh how those lights would dance. Sometimes a waltz. Sometimes a jig. Sometimes just a wave. But always a burst of light. There were days that she watched many individuals and many groups of people enter the woods. It seemed like the more people who entered, the more brilliant the light and the better the dance of lights.

Well, after my grandpa died, she said that she would take walks into the woods. Before my grandpa died, she would just watch from the house. She never visited the tree.

She said maybe that tree could help her, if there is such a tree. One day she walked and walked until she stumbled upon this extremely large tree. She stopped and just looked at the tree. For as far as she could see upward was tree. She was sure that the sky was up there, but seeing with her eyes, there was tree, limbs, leaves and flowers. She stood there looking at this huge tree with its long melon green fern like leaves and soft pink and white flowers. She said that she wondered if this was the tree with the light that shown from the woods at night

 During the daytime, the Sparkle Tree just looked like the other trees. But when she put her hands on the tree, she said that she felt something different. It was as if the tree was inviting her to stay. So, she said that she sat down with her back to the tree, then leaned back on the tree. She said that she had never felt so much comfort before. She just sat there and enjoyed the surroundings and listened to the woods. It was as if the tree was communicating with her to share what she was feeling. So, she stayed and talked and listened for a while. She said that she didn't remember how long she sat, but she was better when she returned home. She said when she left the woods and returned home, she had a joy that she didn't have when she entered the woods. That night she looked towards the woods and there it was, the light from the sparkle tree, a brilliant white. She said the whitest white that she had ever seen. As time passed, she noticed that the light from the forest would be of many colors. She discovered that others had visited the tree. She believed this to explain the various colors from the woods.

She said when you put your problems on the tree, then it soaks it in. The tree then releases its calming power on you. If you take in the power of the tree and it changes your outlook on life, the tree then gets more color changing power and releases it through its flowers. For many years she watched the colors change. Still a vibrant array of colors each night. She said since her discovery of the tree, she has never seen it go dark. She did remember, however, a few years before she journeyed to the woods, that the light did diminish. It didn't go out, but it did lose its vibrancy and expansion. It didn't reach high above the woods anymore neither did it dance like before.

I asked her, what did she think happened? She said that maybe the people didn't respond to the tree positively. Maybe they brought their problems, released them, but didn't receive what the tree had for them. Maybe they just didn't believe. She said you must remember that trees are alive just like you are. What you feed them will determine how they respond. Even though, I know that trees are alive, I never thought of them in such a manner. I guess it's like humans, we respond more effectively with positive behavior rather than negative behavior.

On one of our short breaks from school, we invited two of our friends, yes, Zion and Mary, along to visit grandma. Now, Zion, didn't really like the outdoors, but she liked the stories that we told about our visits to grandma's. Mary, on the other hand, loved the outdoors and especially mud. Her face would light up at the presence of mud. So, Mary was game for whatever happened. We had told them of the many fun days of adventure that we had while visiting grandma. We never told them of the light coming from the woods. So, just before leaving the city to go to grandma's house, my sister and I told them of the light that glows above the woods at night. They didn't believe us at first, but we asked them had we ever lied to them. This reassured them that there was probably some truth to this story. Mary was excited to find out.

As we arrived, they were full of excitement looking for the lights. It was funny to me and my sister, because it was still daylight and they were looking for the lights. So, we reminded them again that the lights are only seen at night. They calmed down. But when nightfall was apparently approaching, we all gathered on the front porch, facing the woods, everyone in her spot to view the amazing light show. When it began, my sister and I watched as our friends faces gleamed with amazement. We listened as they ahhed, and ooed. We snickered silently as they expressed their enthusiasm. We sat there for hours with grandma, just enjoying the scene.

As we entered the house to go to bed, we talked about what we had just viewed. They wanted to know why we had not told them about the lights. Our response, "We didn't think you would believe us then". They just laughed and said, "You're right, we wouldn't". They told us how beautiful the lights were and that they were glad that we shared it with them. They wanted to know what the tree looked like and how does it glow like that. My grandma told them a small portion of the story of the Sparkle Tree. They were so happy that they had come to grandma's house with us. We told them that we had never been far enough into the woods to see the tree that makes the beautiful lights.

Chapter 3

Dimming Lights

Many years have passed since my grandma told me about the sparkle tree. My grandma has also passed on. I'm an adult now and lives in my grandma's house. These days I don't spend much time watching the woods and admiring the light from the tree. I still haven't been deep enough into the woods to see the actual tree. I have walked to the woods to learn of the many great finds that are there. It is quite a distance from the house. The tree still sparkles at night, just a little dim. I do wonder why the light is so dim.

I decided to inquire about this Sparkle Tree. I put an ad in the local paper: *LOOKING FOR INFORMATION ON THE SPARKLE TREE.*

PLEASE CONTACT NANCY REDELL AT 555-2233. A few days passed with no response. As I waited for people to respond to the ad, the light was getting dimmer and dimmer. Weeks passed and the light continued to dim. I was sorely afraid that the light seemed to be going out. I wondered what would happen if the light went out. Would the tree die? Would it just disintegrate? Or even explode? What would happen to the other life in the woods? My mind was going.

As I waited wondering what would happen if the light went out, I could see the lowering and dimmer of the light. Then the phone rang. Hello? Hello, is this NANCY REDELL? Yes, it is I replied. I have some news about the Sparkle Tree the voice stated. Are you sure it's the Sparkle Tree that I'm referring to? I asked. Yes, the voice said, if it's the one far,

far in the woods. That's the one. That's great, I

replied. May I come to talk with you, the voice on

the other end of the phone asked? Sure, I replied.

So, we set up a time to meet to talk about the

sparkle tree.

It was almost nerve wrecking waiting for the day of

the meet. I kept myself busy, mostly watching the

woods at night for the light of the tree. A few days

later there was a knock at the door. It was the

person whose voice was on the phone. We set for

hours talking about the light from the Sparkle Tree.

I told her that I have noticed that the light had

become dim more and more each year. I wanted to

know why. She explained to me that she grew up in

this town and has always lived near the woods, on

one side or the other. She said that the light has

always been there. She also said that there had

never been a time that she could remember that there wasn't a light. So, my question remained. Why is the light so dim? She explained that maybe the tree needs love. Love, I exclaimed. Yes, well it may need what it has been giving all these years.

You see, the tree gives out to everyone that comes to it. It doesn't matter why or when. The Sparkle Tree releases to everyone, but everyone doesn't accept what the tree releases so that the tree can replenish its power to give off such brilliant light. So, what can we do? I asked. She said, we must let people know that when they visit the Sparkle Tree, touch it, talk to it, let it know that you are thankful for the time that it has given to you as you talked about your troubles. Let it know that you feel better and that you will come back again. Most of all we must remember to visit the tree. I thanked her for coming to inform me as how to help a tree that has helped so many others.

It was a great visit. I was so excited! Now, it's time to begin. It was now time for me to go to the tree, the SPARKLE TREE! I wanted to see the whitest white light or even the rainbow of light that soars above the woods. Before going to bed that night, I looked out of the window at the light in the woods. It was still very dim. I slept well that night knowing what I needed to do. I never thought in my life that I would be saving a tree, especially one that exudes light.

Chapter 4

Journey into the Woods

When morning came, I dressed for a long journey. I packed water and lunch. I put on my hat, grabbed a towel and went on an adventure into the woods to find the Sparkle Tree. It was a long walk, but a good walk. As I walked, I envisioned what the tree would look like. Being that I have never seen this tree, only its light above the woods. I had to remember the simple description that was given by my grandma: **a tree with long melon green fern like leaves and soft pink and white flowers**.

As I entered the woods, it was still as amazing as it was the first time, I entered it. More beauty than the last time. I continued my walk. I walked and walked, gazing at the many flowers, bushes, vines, and trees. Listening to the sounds of the many animals communicating in their own way. Listening to their movement from place to place, in the trees and along the ground. Then, there I was, rather there it was, still a way off, towering right in front of me. Its enormous roots emerging from the floor of the woods. Just as I imagined. I was amazed at the sight of it. It was massive. It towered, what seemed to be millions of miles above the floor of the woods. Navigating myself through the roots emerging from the floor of the woods, I continued to walk towards what I believe, from my grandma's description, the Sparkle Tree. Not only did it seem to be a million-mile tower, it was also massive in diameter. It seemed to be as wide as a car on every side.

Gaining my composure, I took a deep breath, then I touched it, The Sparkle Tree. I touched it. I don't know exactly what it felt like to my grandma, but it felt of total excitement, mixed with comfort and relaxation. It made me feel like there were no worries anywhere for anyone. The world is calm, and everyone is resting.

I took my picnic blanket out and placed it on the ground near the tree. Then I took out my water and lunch and placed them on the blanket. I sat down and placed my back against the tree, just like grandma said she did and just talked to the Sparkle Tree. I suddenly realized that the sounds from the animals had quieted. The woods were not without sound, but the communication was lowered as if the population of this community knew what was happening. I guess they knew a counseling session was in progress. I told the Sparkle Tree all about the stories that my grandma had told me about it. I told it all about the lights soaring above the woods and especially about the whitest of white light that she received after her husband died. I stayed for hours just enjoying my surroundings. I felt a sense of peace sitting there. It was as though it helped me to clear my mind. It seemed to also help me to gain a better attitude about situations that I was going through. Clarity, yes clarity. It helped to clear the brain fog.

Before going to bed that night, I looked out the window towards the woods, there it was the whitest of white lights towering above the woods. It looked as though the light was moving, waving, dancing almost. Twinkling! Brilliant! It wasn't dim anymore. It was as if the tree understood everything that I said and felt. I want to believe that my visit made a difference in the brightness of the light of the Sparkle Tree. I decided that night that if no one else would visit the Sparkle Tree, I would visit it once a month. I wouldn't want the light to ever go out. It has changed my life. It gave me a better perspective on the situations that I was facing at that time. I know that it changed my grandma's life for the better. I never saw her sad, even when she talked of my grandpa, she had such a twinkle in her eye and a great smile on her face. When talking about him, she would always look to the woods. It seemed to make her happy.

I decided to place another ad: *IF YOU HAVE EVER VISITED THE SPARKLE TREE, IT NEEDS YOUR HELP. JUST LIKE IT HELPED YOU, IT NEEDS YOUR HELP. THE LIGHT IS DIMMING. PLEASE VISIT TO HELP KEEP THE LIGHT GLOWING.* A few days later, I noticed various cars coming and going. People coming and going most days. Spending hours on hours in the woods. If they noticed me sitting on the porch, going in or going out, they would honk their horn. That made me feel great. I didn't know them, but we all had a common interest, keeping the light in the woods by protecting the light of the Sparkle Tree.

Chapter 5

Night Journey into the Woods

For many nights, I noticed the various colors of lights coming from the woods. There was a plethora of brilliant colors. There were sparkles of light shimmering and dancing through the night. The light was so bright on many nights that I had to close my curtains. I decided then that I would share the story of the sparkle tree with my children and so many other stories that my grandma shared with me. Hopefully my children and others will continue to visit the Sparkle Tree when I am gone. The lights are too beautiful to go out and the tree is too comforting to be destroyed.

Cars and visitors continued to come day after day. Each night the lights are prettier than the night before. I continued to visit the Sparkle Tree each month and it fulfilled me as I continued to visit it. I would find myself in the most relaxed place physically and emotionally whenever I visited the tree. It was almost like a place where time either doesn't exist or flies. Many months passed and the people continued to come, and the lights continued to sparkle and dance.

On one cloudy night as I was sitting on the front porch watching in total awe at the lights above the woods, my eyes ventured lower. I saw a glimmer of light inside the woods. I had never noticed that before. I stood up to see better, as if I could, still being far away. I gazed for a while, wondering what it could be. It looks like light. A fire? Did someone leave something burning? Couldn't be. There's no smoke visually nor smell of smoke.

No one visits the woods after dark. Visitors only come during the day. I decided to go into the woods this night. I had never done this before, never even thought about doing this. I walked off the porch and headed towards the woods. It was really a long walk this time. I was thinking of all the horrible things that could happen to me. Wild animals could attack me. Insects could bite. Snakes could bite me. But none of this had ever happened to me while visiting the woods during the daylight.

As I got closer, I could see the light within the woods better and better. Now I'm curious as to what is going on in these woods. First curiosity, then fear, now I can't believe what I'm seeing. It's a light party going on inside the woods. I always thought that the light came from the top of the trees, but it really begins lower, closer to the floor of the woods. It gets brighter as it gets closer to the top. It was beautiful. No one, to my knowledge, has ever been here during the night. My thoughts were that I am the first person to see the night lights inside the woods. As, I left the woods, I was thinking, this is a must to share. But when, then what would be the repercussions? I decided to wait.

Chapter 6

Night Visits

After thinking it through, I decided to slowly tell people in the community about the lights inside the woods. They had never seen the light inside the woods, because they had only gone inside the woods during the daytime. I told them to come out one night and we'll go in together.

A few nights later a few cars pulled up and blew their horn. We drove closer then got out and walked. As we got closer, I could hear voices yelling that they could see the lights. Many started walking faster and faster. Excited about the great discovery. When we got to the opening of the woods, we stopped. Then we went in, all eyes and mouths open wide. I heard someone say this is so beautiful. They all exclaimed that they never knew this was here.

We stayed and admired the lights inside the woods for many more minutes. As we walked back to the cars, I could hear chatter about the lights and how beautiful the woods looked at night, not only the lights above, but the lights within. Someone asked me if it's like this every night. I replied that I don't know. I had only been within the woods only one night other than tonight.

The knowledge of the lights in the woods at night spread like wildfire! I couldn't believe my eyes. Cars, cars and more cars. People were coming at dust of the day to be inside the woods when night fell. They all wanted to see the lights inside. I didn't go with them; I had already seen the lights. For weeks, people came at dust. Sometimes I wondered if there would be enough room on the inside for all the people. I found it enjoyable to see this support for the Sparkle Tree from so many people.

I heard my grandma say several times, "Be careful what you ask for". I may not have known then what it meant then, but I found out soon. There were so many people coming that I thought all the visits would disrupt my peace and quiet and the population of the woods. Well it was quite a disturbance for a while. Then the number of visitors slowed down. I didn't want the people to stop coming, because I was afraid of the light going out.

Chapter 7

Talk of Destruction

One day as I was sitting on the porch watching my daughter play in the yard, a truck pulled up to the edge of the woods. Two men got out and started looking around. They walked and looked. Then, they turned and walked some more. They then returned to the truck. I couldn't see what was on the side of the truck, because of the distance. Neither could I recognize the men. A few days passed and they were back again. This time with more men and more trucks. Trucks bigger than the first one. This time they went into the woods. They stayed a bit longer than before. I still couldn't see what was going on. So, the next day, I decided to go into town to inquire about what these men were doing in our woods. So, I went into the grocery store. Around here you can always find out what's going on by just talking to people in the grocery store. I found out that they were trying to cut the woods down. This couldn't be. These woods are home to so many animals and plants and the Sparkle Tree. I'm thinking, they can't cut down the Sparkle Tree. This tree is a valuable part of our community.

I went home to think of what could be done to save the woods, or at least the Sparkle Tree. As I sat on the porch thinking about the situation, I thought of a visit where grandma told me of a time when developers wanted to cut the woods down and build some kind of resort or camp or something to bring in more revenue to this community. It was never built. I don't know what stopped it. But I'm sure glad that it didn't happen. I decided to give the newspaper another try.

Here I go again, time to place another ad in the newspaper. But what can I say? First, I need to find out what can be done to stop this from happening. While inquiring, I found out that if we get enough names on a petition to save the Sparkle Tree, we may also be able to stop the cutting of the woods altogether. So, it's time to send the word out in hopes of saving the Sparkle Tree. So, I placed the ad: *IF YOU HAVE EVER VISITED THE SPARKLE TREE, IT NEEDS YOUR HELP. JUST LIKE IT HELPED YOU, IT NEEDS YOUR HELP. THE WOODS ARE ABOUT TO BE DESTROYED AND EVERYTHING IN IT. PLEASE COME TO THE GROCERY STORE AND SIGN THE PETITION TO HELP KEEP THE SPARKLE TREE FROM BEING DESTROYED. WE NEED TO HELP KEEP THE*

LIGHT GLOWING. WE NEED 1000

SIGNATURES BY 5:00 WEDNESDAY.

Chapter 8

Fate of the Sparkle Tree

People came from miles around, daily to sign the petition to keep the Sparkle Tree from being destroyed. There were so many names on the petition, that the section of the woods with the Sparkle Tree was saved. Many of the names on the petition I knew, but most of them I had no idea, from the names who they were. There was one name in particular that I knew but was surprised to see: Mary Micah. It has been years since we had talked. I wondered, why was her name on this petition. How did she know? Come to find out, she had been following the Sparkle Tree for years. Each time a developer wanted to cut the woods down, she stepped in and found them another place to build.

Not knowing, but she was also one of the people who visited the woods during the night. After talking with her weeks later, I learned that she knocked on my door when she made her visit the night, she visited the woods, but unfortunately, I wasn't home. There was no demolition taking place. The homes of the animals and plants were saved also. Our Sparkle Tree was shining brighter than ever, or at least I thought so.

As my daughter grew older, I began to tell her the story that my grandma told me. She had already started to see and wonder about the light above the woods. Her curiosity was being triggered. She began to do as I did. She would gaze out the window when night fell to see the light from the Sparkle Tree shining above the woods. She began to mark on the calendar how the light glimmered and the color of the light each night. Just like me, she had never seen the woods without the light. By the end of the month, she noticed that on most nights, the light was a rainbow of colors.

One night, she finally asked me about the time the men entered the woods. I had not thought that she remembered that incident. I explained to her why they were there and what transpired. I told her that the petition saved the woods and the Sparkle Tree. I also told her that's why people are coming more often and honking their car horns. I hope that I have expressed to my daughter how vital this tree is to this community and to the population of the woods. We must keep these lights glowing at all cost.

As the months went by, people continued to come, and light continued to blaze. One month so many people visited the tree that it triggered an arrangement of movements that I had never seen. it was like the light was dancing to the beat of rock n roll. I received such joy just watching the dance moves of the light. About a year later, letters started coming in. People remembered the ad that I placed about the fate of the Sparkle Tree becoming dim, then how it was about to be destroyed by developers. There were many nights that I would look towards the woods and see cars parked or people standing around admiring the lights. Because the light within the woods was extremely bright, not many people entered the woods at night. We mostly looked from afar at the show above the woods.

There were many stories about how the Sparkle

Tree changed lives in various ways. Individuals and

families would stop by every so often to tell us of

how their lives and or attitude toward life were

changed for the better. We all agreed that the light

inside the woods at night was amazing. But we

totally agreed that the daytime experience with the

Sparkle Tree was the best experience ever, knowing

that when night falls, our skies will be filled with

the brightest and most colorful lights to be seen for

miles and miles.

I really miss my grandma and the stories she told. I

am thankful though, that she shared the story of the

Sparkle Tree with me. I saw what this tree did for

my grandma and I know what it has done for me. I

hope that my daughter will continue this tradition of telling her children about the Sparkle Tree. Just like I believe that this tree with its lights brought comfort and joy to grandma, it also brought me comfort like no other.

ABOUT THE AUTHOR

Stefenie is a wife, mother, and grandmother who loves God, her family, the arts, and gardening. She was born to Nancy "Redell" Moore and George Eddie Lucas in Greenwood, Mississippi. She was raised by her mom and her grandfather Ben Moore. She is married to Pastor Albert Lott. They have six children between them, two girls and four boys. They also have twelve grandchildren. Stefenie is the eldest of five brothers and three sisters. She also has a stepsister who preceded her in death. She has been in education as a teacher for over thirty years and has recently retired. She serves as the copastor of Soul Winners for Christ, where she leads praise and worship service, teaches Sunday school, and facilitates Bible Study. She's the founder and director of Academics Academy Extended Learning Program. She also lives on a farm, where she grows vegetables and herbs. Stefenie advocates eating safe and healthy. She loves singing, dancing, teaching, and teaching about the health benefits of herbs and how to grow vegetables with little effort. Stefenie believes God to be her source. She not only believes in God but also believes God.